KATIE MORAG
OF
COURSE!

Mairi Hedderwick

Saturday Sweets

'It is Grandmother's Day next Sunday,' Mrs McColl reminded Katie Morag McColl and her little brother Liam one Wednesday morning. 'Grandma Mainland is off on holiday in Australia but Grannie Island has invited us over for tea. What will you give her for a present?'

'Sweeties!' chorused Katie Morag and Liam, immediately.

'Which kind do you think she would like?' queried Mr McColl, who ran the village shop on the Isle of Struay. He took great pride in filling all his sweetie jars with the latest supplies that came on the big boat from the mainland.

There were
peppermint
balls, sherbet dabs,
long liquorice laces,
gobstoppers,
caramel
chews and
chocolate bears, to
name but a few.

'We'll just have to
taste them all and then
choose,' said Katie Morag, looking
ever so seriously at her mother and
father. Liam agreed. He always
agreed with his big sister when he
knew she was on to a good thing.

Katie Morag and Liam were only
allowed to spend part of their pocket
money on sweets on a Saturday.

They saved the rest in their piggybanks. That was the McColl family  rule. Sometimes it was hard waiting for Saturday to come. But then it made Saturday such a special day. Katie Morag would spend all week choosing her bagful of sweeties in her head, sometimes changing her mind at the last minute and worrying if she had made the right choice. Some sweets could be such a disappointment.

On this particular week, Saturday could not come soon enough, because she and Liam would have the added excitement of choosing sweeties for Grannie Island, too.

And because of the special occasion, Mr and Mrs McColl had agreed that Katie Morag and Liam would have to spend all their pocket money on sweets, just this once. What a sweetie spree!

On the Friday, Katie Morag raked through the recycle bin at school for something special to hold all the sweeties that Grannie was going to have. She found an empty chocolate box.  **Perfect!**

The teacher said she could have it when she told him the reason. 'Lucky Grannie Island!' he smiled.

'We'll get lots of sweeties for Grannie in there,' she told Liam, when she got home and hid the box under her bed. 'Now we must make her a card.' Katie Morag drew a picture of Grannie Island on her

tractor and Liam stuck loveheart stickers all round the edges. 'BIG decision day!' smiled Mrs McColl next morning when she gave Katie Morag and Liam their pocket money.

Mr McColl took down sweetie
jars from the shelf and put them on
the counter.

'Don't take too long,' he warned.
Saturday was a busy day in the
shop and the islanders were
queuing up behind Katie Morag
and Liam. They didn't take long.

They ordered one of every kind and more of the same until all their money was gone.

Racing up to their bedroom, Katie Morag and Liam started the difficult job of tasting each sweet and trying to decide which ones would go into Grannie's box, which lay empty on Katie Morag's bed. It took all afternoon. Katie Morag

and Liam could not agree on which ones Grannie would like best. They knew the ones THEY liked best – the gobstoppers, the caramel chews and the chocolate bears.

'Grannie would choke on gobstoppers and caramel chews would be bad for the fillings in her teeth,' said Katie Morag.

'And the chocolate bears are really for children,' added Liam. Soon all the gobstoppers, caramel chews and chocolate bears were finished.

The remaining sweets had to be tasted again to make quite sure 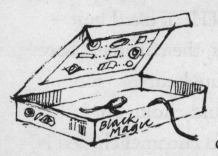 they were the right ones for Grannie. By teatime it was all over. You've guessed it – all the sweeties were gone, except for one long liquorice lace. Katie Morag put it in the very empty box back under the bed. She was feeling awful, in more ways than one.

Not surprisingly, Katie Morag and Liam were not at all hungry at teatime even though it was their favourite: sausages, beans, fried mushrooms and mashed tatties. They certainly did not want any cake or pudding.

Grannie was over for tea. 'I bet you two have eaten far too many sweeties today,' she said. Katie Morag and Liam hung their heads. Oh dear, oh dear!

It was Grandmother's Day TOMORROW! What would they do?

That night in bed Katie Morag thought and thought. She knew she couldn't ask for more money. And she couldn't wait until next Saturday. Oh, it would be the easiest thing in the world to do without sweeties next week just to be able to give Grannie her present. But next week would be too late.

Katie Morag even thought in
her sleep and in the morning she
came up with the answer.

'We will each give Grannie one
of our favourite things,' she told
Liam when she woke him up. 'And
it must be something we bought
with our own money.' Liam
reluctantly agreed.

Choosing items to go into the box took nearly as long as eating all the sweets the previous day. Liam found it very difficult to make up his mind but found it easier when Katie Morag explained that he would always be able to play with his little wind-up car whenever he went over to Grannie's house.

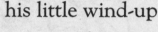

Katie Morag

chose her miniature pony with its very own tiny brush for brushing its mane and tail. She draped

the long liquorice lace round the
pony's neck like reins and
sellotaped the box shut.

After breakfast Katie Morag and
Liam set off as fast as they could
for Grannie Island's on the other
side of the bay.

ISLE OF STRUAY SHOP & P.O.
Thank you!

The rest of the McColl family were coming along later. Katie Morag wanted to get there as soon as possible before her parents saw that there was no big box of sweets for Grannie. Maybe Mr and Mrs McColl would think Grannie had eaten them all by the time they got there?

'Happy Grandmother's Day, Grannie!' sang Katie Morag and Liam as they came through Grannie's back door. 'Here's your present!'

'Chocolates!' Grannie smiled.

But she was just being nice because Grannie Island doesn't like chocolates very much. 'Er, well, no,' mumbled Katie Morag. 'Open the box,' demanded Liam, desperate to see his little car.

When she did, Grannie gave a
big smile. 'What a dear wee little
car! Thanks! Can you show me
how it works, Liam?' Liam was
down on the floor in seconds, as
you can imagine. 'And Katie
Morag – a little pony! Thank you!
That reminds me, I have been
thinking of getting
a real pony. What
do you think?'

It was Katie
Morag's turn to smile
a really big smile.
'I think that is a
WONDERFUL idea!'

'I'm not much of a
one for sweeties,'
said Grannie,
unwinding the

reins off the pony, 'but I do love a piece of liquorice now and again.'

By the time Mr and Mrs McColl and the baby got to Grannie's everyone was in high spirits and they didn't mind at all that all the sweeties had obviously been eaten already.

Katie Morag secretly vowed that
from then on she would get two
liquorice laces every Saturday for
Grannie out of her own sweetie
money. She told Liam the secret.
He agreed.

Liam always agrees with his big
sister when he knows she is on to a
good thing.

The Pony
and the Hamster

The day Grannie Island's pony
came to the island everyone was
down at the pier to see it arrive.
Katie Morag was right at the front,
craning her neck, waiting for the
boat to appear round the headland.

'Here she comes!' shouted Katie Morag. The captain of the *Lady of the Isles* let out a blast from the ship's hooter in reply. Everyone cheered.

Katie Morag's friend Agnes was expecting something special off the boat, too. It was her birthday present. It was a hamster.

'In a golden cage and it will be mine, all mine!' Agnes crowed.

Katie Morag could not show off in the same kind of way, for it wasn't really her pony, but she was equally excited.

'I'll ride the pony, won't I?' Katie Morag loudly reminded her grandmother. Agnes couldn't have a ride on a hamster, that was for sure. 'I bet the pony is shiny black all over with the longest mane and tail ever!' Katie Morag boasted, as the boat was tied up. 'I'll call her Beauty and I'll ride over to you at High Farm, Agnes!'

'He is called Eriska,'
said Grannie Island, quietly,
'and he is mottled grey and
white. I think he will need
a lot of brushing. He has
been neglected.'

Katie Morag tried
not to show her
disappointment. She wondered
what 'neglected' meant.

A high crane swung over with a
great wooden box hanging from a
large hook. Inside the box, its head
sticking out, was the pony. It
looked terrified at being so high up
in the air. The whites of its eyes
were showing and its nostrils were
flaring. Over and above the
screeching of the boat's winch
and the hubbub of the islanders'

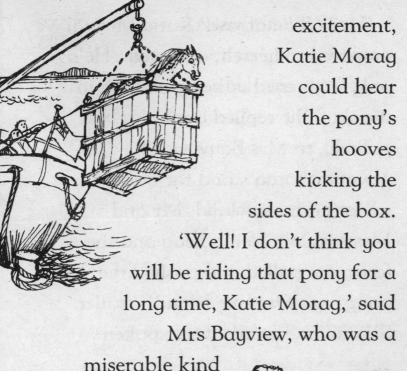

excitement,
Katie Morag
could hear
the pony's
hooves
kicking the
sides of the box.
'Well! I don't think you
will be riding that pony for a
long time, Katie Morag,' said
Mrs Bayview, who was a
miserable kind
of a person.

'I will! Tomorrow!' Katie Morag muttered to herself, annoyed. 'He's only frightened at being so high in the sky,' she replied out loud, but politely, to Mrs Bayview.

Katie Morag stood far back whilst Grannie Island, Mr and Mrs McColl, Neilly Beag and the ferryman pulled and pushed the pony onto Grannie Island's trailer. Several bad words were spoken.

The McColl family followed
Grannie's tractor and trailer in
their Land Rover. Katie Morag sat
sadly in the back; she had thought
she would be riding over on the
back of Eriska.

Getting the pony out of the trailer
was easier than expected. Pleased to
be on dry land, he let Grannie
Island lead him to the stable where
a bucket of bran mash was waiting.
He gave a happy sort of snort but
there was still a little bit of the
whites of his eyes showing.

'Can't I ride him
now?' asked
Katie Morag,
hopefully.

'Not yet,' answered Mr McColl. 'Eriska was not treated well in his previous home. He is wary of humans. But you can help to settle him; that way he'll get to know you.'

So every day Katie Morag went over to Grannie's and helped with the chores, hoping that *that* day would be the day she could climb

on Eriska's back. She forgot all about Agnes and certainly did not want her around. There was much to do. The stable had to be swept and hosed, and, as it was early spring,

fresh hay put in the rack. Katie
Morag dug up carrots, filled the
trough with water and mixed the
bran mash in Eriska's bucket. Soon
he was calm enough to stand whilst
Grannie Island and Katie Morag
brushed him all over. That was
when he got an apple, which he
loved. Eriska also loved
Polo mints.

   He was allowed one if he came
across the field when he was called.
Soon he was racing across
whenever he saw Katie Morag at
the gate. Katie Morag loved the feel

of Eriska's muzzle delicately taking the mint from her outstretched hand.

'I think he likes you,' Grannie Island would smile.

'So can I have a ride today?' Katie Morag would ask.

After asking the same question every day for a whole week and always being told 'not yet', she soon got bored and didn't bother to go to Grannie's any more. A pony was an awful lot of hard work.

She went over to High Farm instead and played with Agnes and Hammie, who was a very friendly, if grubby, hamster. Katie Morag forgot all about Eriska. Until the dreadful day she found Agnes crying sore in her bedroom. Her

mother had told her that the
hamster was going back on the next
boat to the pet shop on the
mainland. 'Why?' worried Katie
Morag, comforting her friend.

'Because she hasn't cleaned out
its cage for a week,' said Mrs
McMaster, sternly. 'And I'm the
one who feeds it and IT IS NOT
MY HAMSTER!'

Being a farmer's wife, Mrs McMaster had umpteen other animals and birds to look after. She was not in a good mood. She slammed out of the door shouting, 'Neglect, that is what it is, neglect. You are not responsible enough to have any pets!'

Hearing these harsh words, Katie Morag suddenly remembered Eriska. She took to her heels and ran all the way over to Grannie's as fast as she could. The stable was empty. It needed a clean. Katie Morag set to with brush and hose. She rattled through all the other chores. She polished Eriska's saddle like never before.

Eriska was in his field. He lifted his head when he saw her come to

the gate but
then went on
eating the
grass. No matter
how she called and
waved Polo mints at him he took
no notice.

It was Katie
Morag's turn to
start blubbing.
She slumped
down in a heap,
stuffing all the
Polo mints into

her mouth and didn't hear Grannie Island coming across the yard, Eriska's saddle over her arm.

'I think he thought you were not coming back,' said Grannie, gently. 'But look, he's coming over now.'

Eriska came slowly over to Katie Morag and put his head down for her to scratch his favourite itchy bit behind his left ear and didn't mind there being no Polo mints left. 'Now I know he really likes you,' smiled Grannie Island. And then she said, 'I think it is time for your first ride, Katie Morag!'

How wonderful to be so high and to feel Eriska's movements beneath her! Katie Morag did not mind Grannie Island leading with the

rein. They went all round the big
field. It was a beginning ride and it
was FANTASTIC!

'You sit very well,' praised
Grannie Island. 'Next time, you
will take the reins!'

'And then can I go over to
Agnes's and can she have a ride?
I'm going to help her look after
Hammie. Can she help look
after Eriska?'

'That sounds a very good idea,'
said Grannie Island.
'But now it is time
for tea. We'll give
Eriska his bucket
of mash first.'

And she lifted
Katie Morag off
Eriska and gave
her a big hug.

The Camping Holiday

Every day of the summer holidays
Katie Morag rode over on Eriska
to play with her friend Agnes at
High Farm.

Agnes and her family, however, had to go to the mainland for a few days. They asked Katie Morag to feed Hammie, Agnes's hamster. Just as before, she would ride over on Eriska. It would be no bother.

But when the Big Boy Cousins arrived on the island for their camping holiday the very day Agnes left, things got complicated. Katie Morag wanted to go camping, too.

The big decision was where to pitch the tent. 'Away from Grannie's,' whispered Hector, the biggest Boy Cousin, who was at secondary school. 'We'll get chores to do, otherwise.'

'Not at Castle McColl. It's too scary,' shuddered Murdo Iain, one of the twins.

'We can't be too far away from High Farm,' remembered Katie Morag and she told them why. The Big Boy Cousins all sighed but they pored over the Isle of Struay map searching for the best spot.

'Look!' pointed Archie, who was good at map reading. 'Heading north-west from High Farm and past Heron Wood there is a bay called Pig's Paradise. It will be perfect!'

Grannie agreed. 'Yes, that is a good place to camp. Just remember the tides; but Katie Morag knows all about that.' She said they could load the camping gear onto Eriska. She packed peanut butter and jam sandwiches to give them strength for the long hike over to the other side of the island.

Pig's Paradise was perfect. Soft white sand fringed the beach. Turquoise blue water stretched out to a small island covered in sea pinks with a cave hidden in its cliffs. There was not a house in sight. The cousins could shriek and yell to their hearts' content.

Soon the tent was up and driftwood had been collected for the barbecue.

After
supper the
cousins built
an enormous
sandcastle
at the edge
of the sea.
Water soon
filled the moat. And then it was
time to snuggle into their sleeping
bags. Everyone slept soundly.

Next morning the sandcastle and
its moat had disappeared. 'It was
the tide,' explained Katie Morag,
who knew about things the Big Boy
Cousins did not, they being from a
big city. 'At one time in the day
the tide brings the sea closer to the
land; half a day later the tide takes
the sea further away.'

But the Big Boy Cousins were not listening. They were planning an expedition to the island.

'I have to go to High Farm to feed Hammie,' remembered Katie Morag, reluctantly. Jamie said he would keep her company.

'Then we can ride over together. Bareback!' she replied, cheering up.

'Like wild Highlanders!' whooped Jamie, picking up crow feathers.

They stuck the black feathers in
their hair and painted charcoal
patterns on their faces using the
cold ash from last night's fire. As
they set off on Eriska they haloo-ed

to the others, who were already
starting to swim to the island.
'Have the supper ready for the
Struay Chiefs!' they shouted
and galloped off.

It began to rain heavily. Katie
Morag and Jamie soon dried out at
High Farm. They fed Hammie and
let him have a romp around in
Agnes's bedroom before putting
him back into his cage. They went
down to the sitting room
and tried to finish
off Mrs McMaster's
jigsaw, waiting for
the rain to stop.

Over at the island the others
climbed up the cliffs in the
downpour and danced on the top,
seagull feathers and seaweed stuck
in their dripping hair. They called
themselves the Castaway Kings. On
the way back down they found the
cave near the water's edge. It was
dark but dry. Deep inside, at the
back, it was cluttered with sea junk
and bone-dry driftwood.

When they had explored enough
they found that the water around
the island was, strangely, so
shallow they could paddle all the
way back to the beach. They played
rounders, splashing each other with
spray from the bat and the ball. It
was great to be so wet and no
grown-ups saying, 'Come inside, at
once!' Nobody had thought,
however, to cover the wood pile
and when it came time to get the
fire going for supper the wood was
too wet. Cold beans were all right,
but raw tatties and sausages were
not. A cold wind was beginning to
blow, as well.

'There's dry wood in the cave,'
remembered Dougal. 'We could go
and cook in there.'

It was fun wading back through
the now choppy waves, each cousin
carrying a plate, a fork and a bag
of food. Archie took extra plates

and forks for Katie Morag and
Jamie. Hector had the matches and
the frying pan.

It wasn't long before there was a
good blaze going at the back of the
cave and the sausages were sizzling.
The cave was warm and full of
golden shadows.

On the way back from High Farm
Katie Morag and Jamie urged
Eriska on fast, looking forward to
their supper.

When the Castaway Kings saw
the Struay Chiefs returning, they
yelled, 'Come on over! Your supper
is here!'

Katie Morag tied Eriska to one of
the tent pegs.

The water was up to their knees
as Katie Morag
and Jamie
waded over,
but Katie
Morag

hardly noticed in the excitement of going across to the island.

How cosy it was in the cave; the food was delicious. 'We'll wait till the rain stops before we go back,' said Hector, being sensible. Katie Morag agreed.

She should have known
better. It wasn't until water
came seeping in at the
mouth of the cave that she
remembered about the tide.

'Quick! We must get back
to the beach!' she cried. But
it was too late. The water
was too deep to wade. And
too wild to swim across, for
the tide had brought with it
a strong current which the
cousins could see swirling
around the island.

'Eriska! He's higher and stronger
than the waves,' cried Katie Morag.
'Eriska! Eriska!' she called.
He heard her and obediently
plodded towards the beach – taking
the tent with him. It collapsed as

Eriska strained to get free. Sleeping
bags, clothes and rucksacks
tumbled out into the rain. With a
'thwang' the tent peg and guy
rope parted company and Eriska
plunged into the sea.

Six times Eriska ploughed
through the waves, three times with
two terrified cousins clinging to his
mane, their legs dangling into the
sea; three times without. Katie
Morag and Jamie stayed till last to
give Eriska encouragement.

It was a bedraggled bunch of
Struay Chiefs and Castaway Kings
and their trusty steed that arrived
at Grannie Island's just as it was
getting dark. They were soaked to
the skin, their feathers bent, their
faces smudged with streaks of
charcoal.

'WHAT ON EARTH!?'

she exclaimed, when she opened
the door.

Katie Morag and the Big Boy Cousins told Grannie all about the disaster of the wet wood and the tent falling down as they jostled round her warm kitchen stove.

They said nothing about the island and the tide. It didn't seem so terrible now that they were safe. The Big Boy Cousins had learned an important lesson about the sea that they would never ever forget.

Grannie stoked up the fire. 'Hot baths for everyone,' she ordered, 'but before you take off your wet things, out you all go and give Eriska a good rub down. And get that seaweed out of his tail! How on earth did it get there?'

The cousins, damp though they were, did not complain. They headed for the stable, keen to give Eriska his best ever rubbing down.

'And I'll give him the biggest apple I can find,' declared Katie Morag, 'and a WHOLE packet of Polo mints!' Eriska had saved the day, after all.

Later that night as Katie Morag, warm and glowing after her bath, lay in her grandmother's bed she could hear the Big Boy Cousins sleepily whispering in the room next door.

'We'll have to salvage the camping gear tomorrow,' muttered Hector.

'Let's pitch the tent right beside High Farm,' suggested Jamie.

'Good idea,' thought Katie Morag as she drifted off to sleep. 'Agnes will be home soon. She will like that.'